Heaps of happiness!

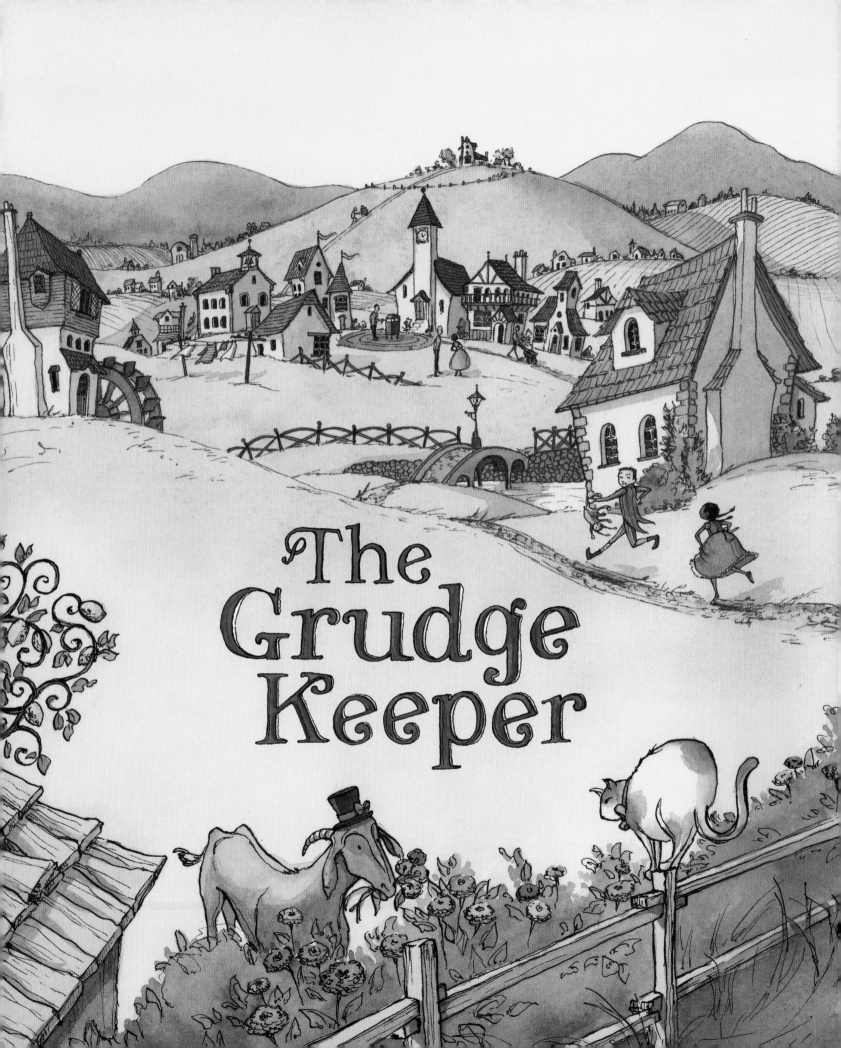

The Grudge Keeper

For Doug, who doesn't
—*M. R.*

To my Wheeler family: Nancy, Wayne, and Pat
—*E. W.*

Published by
PEACHTREE PUBLISHERS
1700 Chattahoochee Avenue
Atlanta, Georgia 30318-2112
www.peachtree-online.com

Text © 2014 by Mara Rockliff
Illustrations © 2014 by Eliza Wheeler

Book and cover design by Eliza Wheeler
Illustrations created with dip pens, India ink, and watercolor on 140 lb.
cold-pressed 100% rag archival paper. Title is hand lettered. Text is typeset
in Baskerville Infant Roman.

Printed in October 2016 by Imago in China
10 9 8 7 6 5 4

Library of Congress Cataloging-in-Publication Data

Rockliff, Mara.
  The Grudge Keeper / written by Mara Rockliff ; illustrated by Eliza
Wheeler. – First edition.
     pages cm
  Summary: "No one in the town of Bonnyripple ever kept a grudge, except
old Cornelius, the Grudge Keeper. When Cornelius is nearly buried under
all of the grudges, the townspeople must put their differences aside to save
him."—Provided by publisher.
  ISBN 978-1-56145-729-8
  [1. Forgiveness—Fiction. 2. City and town life—Fiction.] I. Wheeler, Eliza,
illustrator. II. Title.
  PZ7.R5887Gr 2014
  [E]—dc23
                                        2012048880

The Grudge Keeper

written by Mara Rockliff   illustrated by Eliza Wheeler

PEACHTREE
ATLANTA

No one in the town of Bonnyripple ever kept a grudge.
No one, that is, except old Cornelius, the Grudge Keeper.

Ruffled feathers, petty snits, minor tiffs and major huffs,
insults, umbrage, squabbles, dust-ups, and imbroglios—the
Grudge Keeper received them all, large and small, tucking
each one carefully away in his ramshackle cottage.

When Minnie Fletcher's goat gulped down
Elvira Bogg's prizewinning zinnias, Elvira marched
right over to the Grudge Keeper to file a complaint.

When mischievous Sylvester Quincy snagged
the schoolmaster's toupee, the schoolmaster took
terrible offense—straight to Cornelius.

When Big Otto stomped on
Lily Belle's new shoes at the spring
fling, she limped off to Cornelius
and flung her accusations at his feet.

As time went by, the grudges piled up.
They filled the fireplace. They overflowed the tub.
Cornelius jammed them and crammed them into
every crack and corner, but they kept on coming.

Then, one day, the wind rose.

At first, it was a gentle breeze. Laundry fluttered on the lines. Lily Belle's best flowered bonnet skipped away. Big Otto captured it and brought it back, but Lily Belle just grumbled that the petals were all out of place.

Soon the wind grew stronger. Shutters
shook and cupboards rattled. Minnie Fletcher's
fresh-baked lemon pie slid off the windowsill
and landed on Elvira's cat.

The wind ran riot through the schoolhouse,
overturning inkpots and hurling chalk.
The schoolmaster's toupee flew off
his head and sailed outside,
where Minnie Fletcher's
goat gobbled it up.

Night fell, but no candle would stay lit.

The people huddled with their grudges in the darkness,

listening to the hissing, howling,

creaking, crashing,

moaning, groaning,

whistling wind.

At last, the wind

sputtered,

slowed,

and stopped.

The townspeople crept out into the morning light. Clutching their new grudges, they set off for the Grudge Keeper's cottage.

But what was this?

The wind had mixed and mingled, tossed and turned, tumbled and jumbled, and finally dumped the rumpled, crumpled grudges in one whopping pile.

Nothing was where it should be.

Squabbles were scrambled with quibbles. Low blows rested high up in the pile. High dudgeon had drifted down low. And the left-handed compliments had landed on the right-hand side.

The townspeople crowded around the mountain of grudges, pushing, grabbing, shoving, shouting, "Give me that!" "Me first!" and "Mine!"

In the hubbub, no one heard the feeble groan that squeezed out from the bottom of the pile. No one but Sylvester Quincy.

"It's Cornelius!" he cried.

Cornelius? The shouts and shoving stopped. Why hadn't anybody thought to wonder where the Grudge Keeper had gone?

Sylvester Quincy dove in first. Slowly, the others followed suit. Grudges scattered like confetti as they worked to dig Cornelius out of the pile.

Minnie Fletcher found a grudge labeled *Goats Who Make Pigs of Themselves*. Holding it out to Elvira, she said, "I'm sorry about your zinnias."

Elvira looked at her old, worn-out grudge. "What do I need with that?" she said, and fed the grudge to Minnie Fletcher's goat.

The schoolmaster smoothed out a snit called *Sassy,*
Spitball-Spraying Schoolboys. He glanced at Sylvester Quincy.

Then, with a shrug, he rolled it up again and flung it far away.

"I found a bone to pick," Big Otto said to Lily Belle.

"I think it's yours."

Lily Belle blushed and tossed the bone to the pet peeves.

Cornelius staggered to his feet and
stared around. "The grudges!" he cried.
"Where have they all gone?"

Big Otto eyed Elvira Bogg. Minnie Fletcher sneaked
a guilty look at Lily Belle. The schoolmaster shuffled his feet.
Tiffs and huffs, squabbles and quibbles—all the grudges
had been tossed away, down to the last small scrap of pique.

Not a single grudge remained.

Suddenly, with a yowl, Elvira's cat shot through the crowd.

Elvira stumbled into Minnie Fletcher.

Minnie crashed into Big Otto.

And Big Otto toppled over, right on top of Lily Belle.

Cornelius stood ready to receive the grudges.

But they didn't come.

Instead, Minnie helped Elvira to her feet.

"Nice bumping into you," she said.

"I've fallen for you, Lily Belle," Big Otto said.
"Please marry me."

Lily Belle laughed. "I guess I've fallen for you too."

Everyone cheered—except the schoolmaster,
who scowled at Sylvester Quincy. "Don't think I didn't
see you pulling that cat's tail," he said.

And then he winked.

Everyone in town turned out for the big wedding.
Elvira Bogg sneaked cake under the table until
Minnie Fletcher grinned and told her, "You can't
get my goat!"

And when Big Otto waltzed his brand-new
bride into the punch bowl, Lily Belle just giggled.

"You're not mad?" he asked.

"Of course I am!" she said. "Mad about you."

For no one in the town of Bonnyripple ever kept a grudge…

Not even Cornelius.

What with overflowing cupboards full of friendliness, shelves stuffed with smiles, and tabletops heaped high with hugs, he simply didn't have the room.